god bless the gargoyles

story and paintings by

dav pilkey

harcourt brace & company
san diego new york london

 Library of Congress Cataloging-in-Publication
Data. Pilkey, Dav, 1966– God bless the gargoyles/Dav Pilkey. p. cm. Summary: Relates
a rhyming tale about misunderstood gargoyles and the angels who bring solace to
them and to all creatures who are rejected and unloved. ISBN 0-15-200248-0
[1. Gargoyles—Fiction. 2. Angels—Fiction. 3. Stories in rhyme.] I. Title.
PZ8.3.P55867Go 1996 [E]—dc20 95-2467 First edition A B C D E

The paintings in this book were
made with acrylics, watercolors, and India ink.

Printed in Singapore

For Cindy, Dave, Aaron, and Connor Mancini

in a long-ago time, when long-ago peoples
were building cathedrals and raising up steeples,
they crafted stone creatures and set them on perches
to guard and protect and watch over the churches.

so gargoyles were born, and they stood night and day,
keeping evil and terrible spirits away.
and ne'er was a creature so true and so loyal
as the watchful, courageous, and fearless gargoyle.

but the years came and went, and the people did, too.
and in time, they forgot what their ancestors knew.
and whenever they passed by the gargoyles' lairs,
they trembled in fear at the gargoyles' stares.

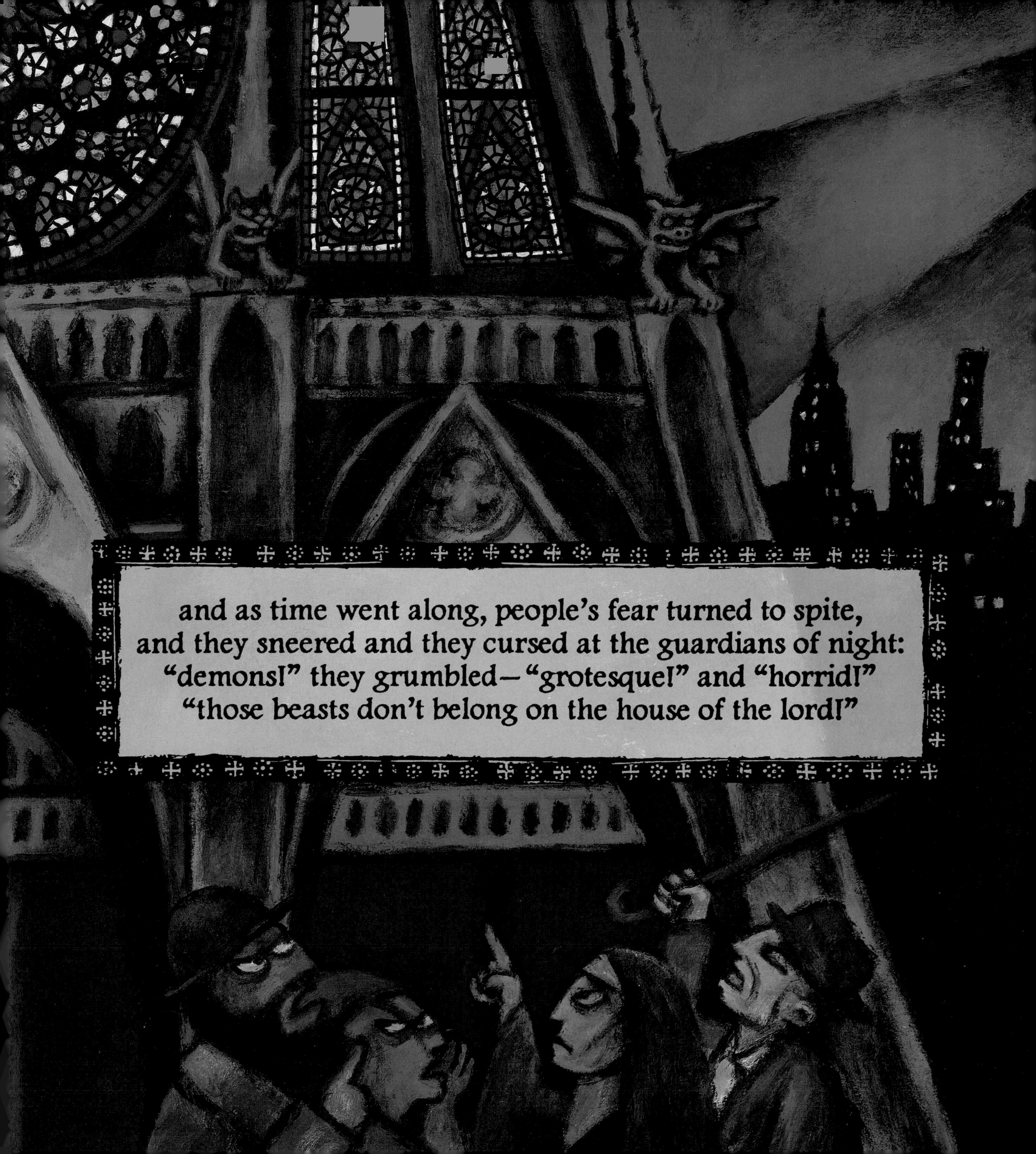
and as time went along, people's fear turned to spite,
and they sneered and they cursed at the guardians of night:
"demons!" they grumbled—"grotesque!" and "horrid!"
"those beasts don't belong on the house of the lord!"

when the gargoyles heard these words that were spoken,
their stony old hearts became crumbled and broken.
then storms rumbled in, and their eyes filled with rain,
and in stillness they stayed, alone and in pain.

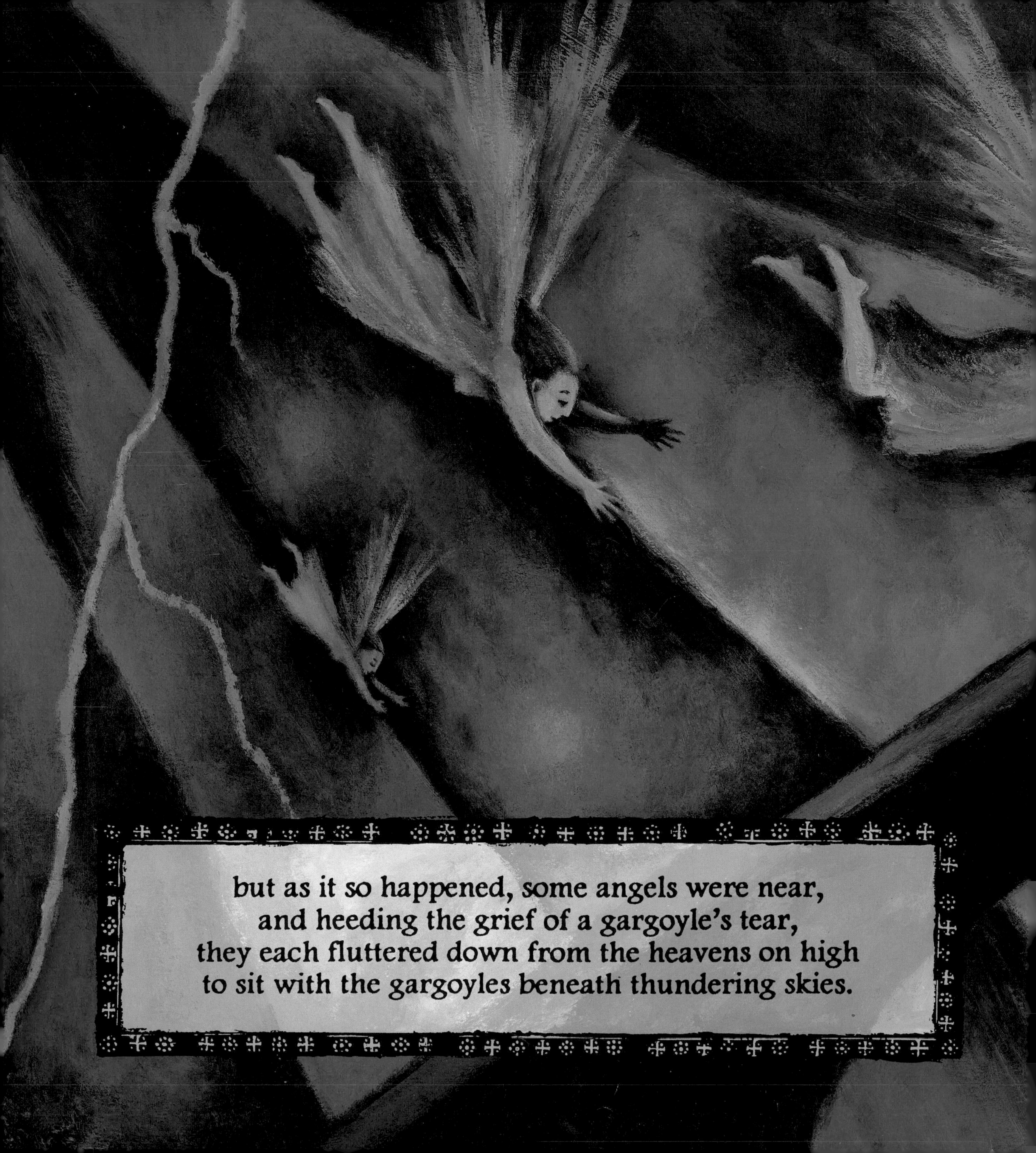

but as it so happened, some angels were near,
and heeding the grief of a gargoyle's tear,
they each fluttered down from the heavens on high
to sit with the gargoyles beneath thundering skies.

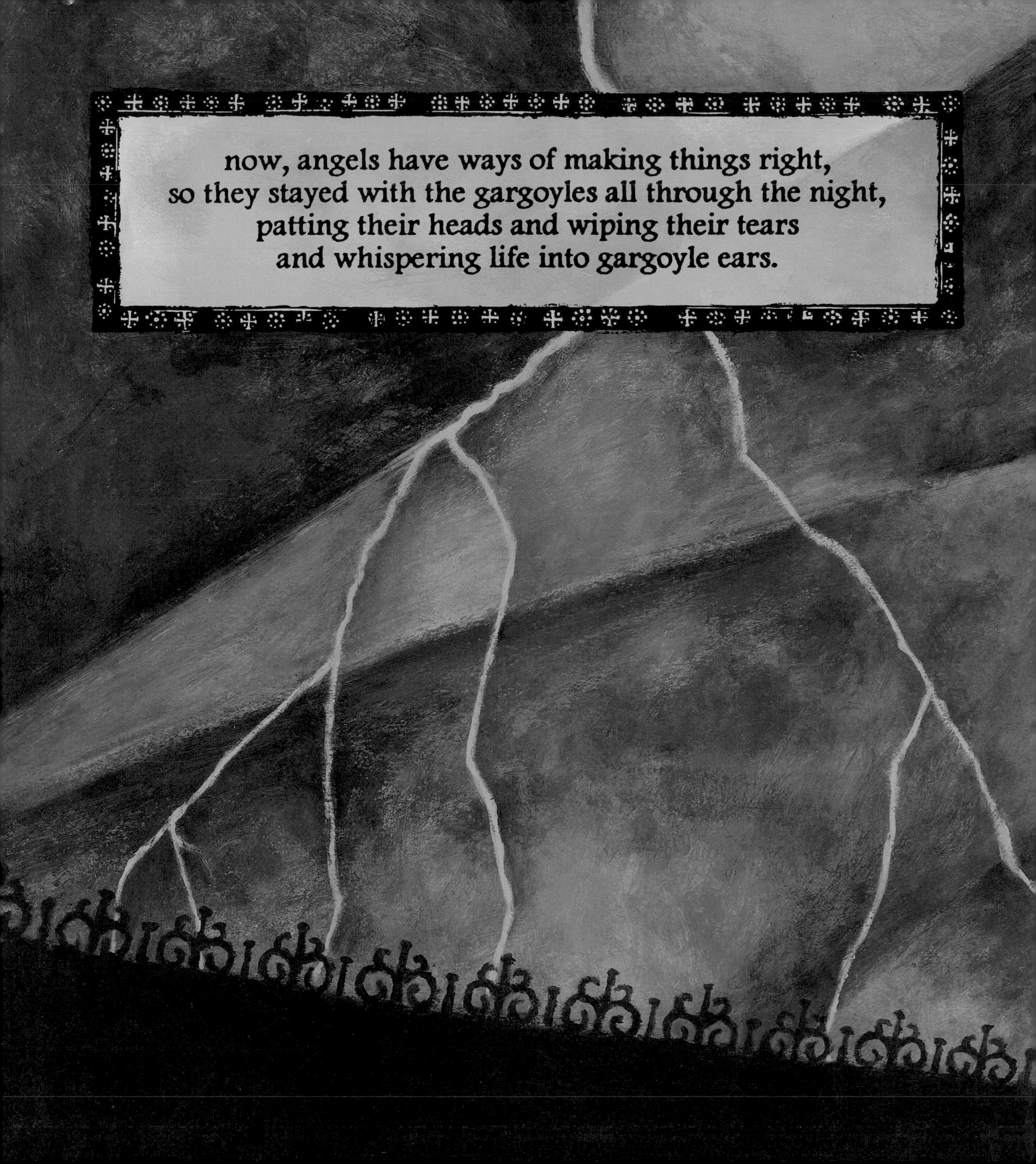

now, angels have ways of making things right,
so they stayed with the gargoyles all through the night,
patting their heads and wiping their tears
and whispering life into gargoyle ears.

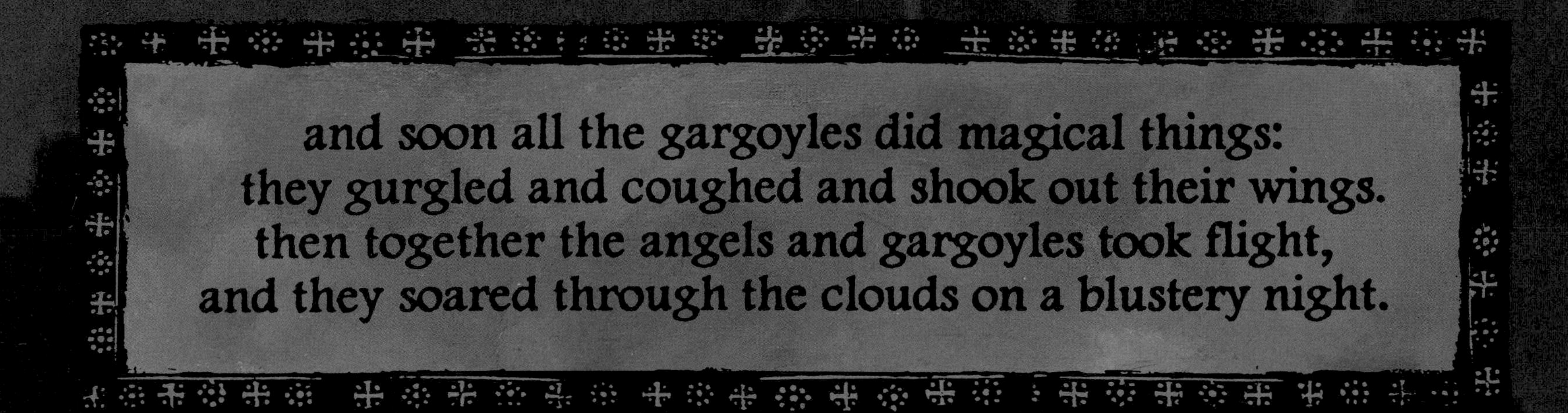

and soon all the gargoyles did magical things:
they gurgled and coughed and shook out their wings.
then together the angels and gargoyles took flight,
and they soared through the clouds on a blustery night.

and while over pastures and hills they were winging,
the voices of angels were radiantly singing
music of healing and songs of rebirth
to all of the creatures in all of the earth:

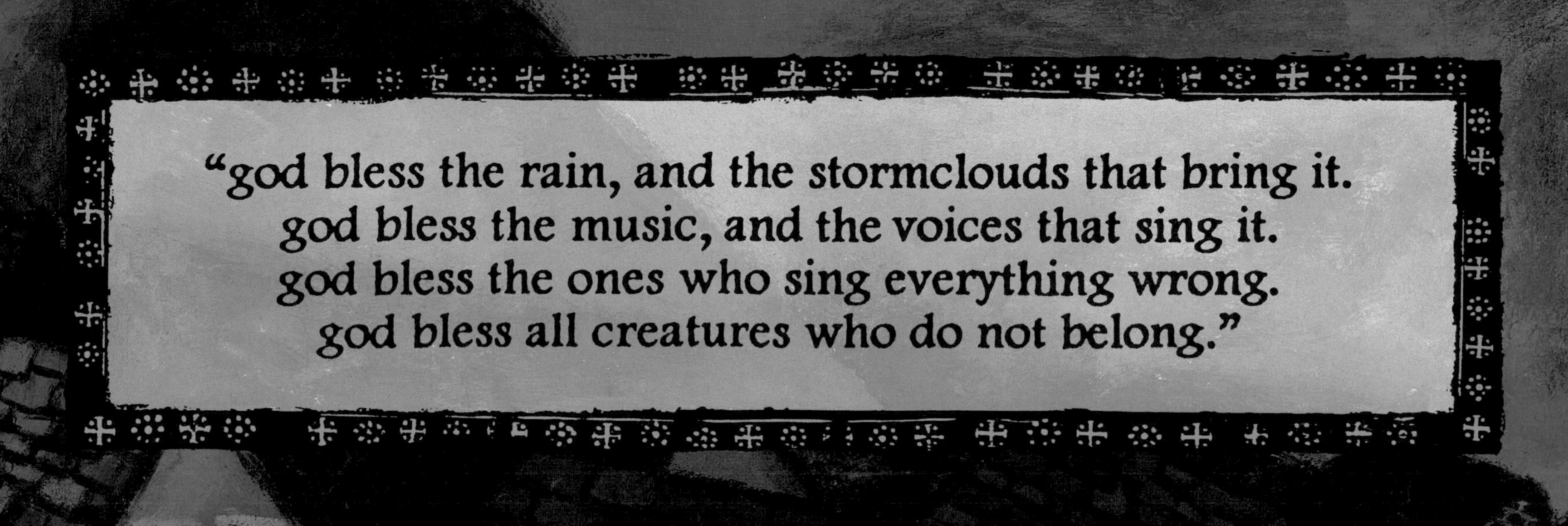

"god bless the rain, and the stormclouds that bring it.
god bless the music, and the voices that sing it.
god bless the ones who sing everything wrong.
god bless all creatures who do not belong."

"god bless the hearts and the souls who are grieving
for those who have left, and for those who are leaving.
god bless each perishing body and mind,
god bless all creatures remaining behind."

"god bless the dreamers whose dreams have awoken.
god bless the lovers whose hearts have been broken.
god bless each soul that is tortured and taunted,
god bless all creatures alone and unwanted."

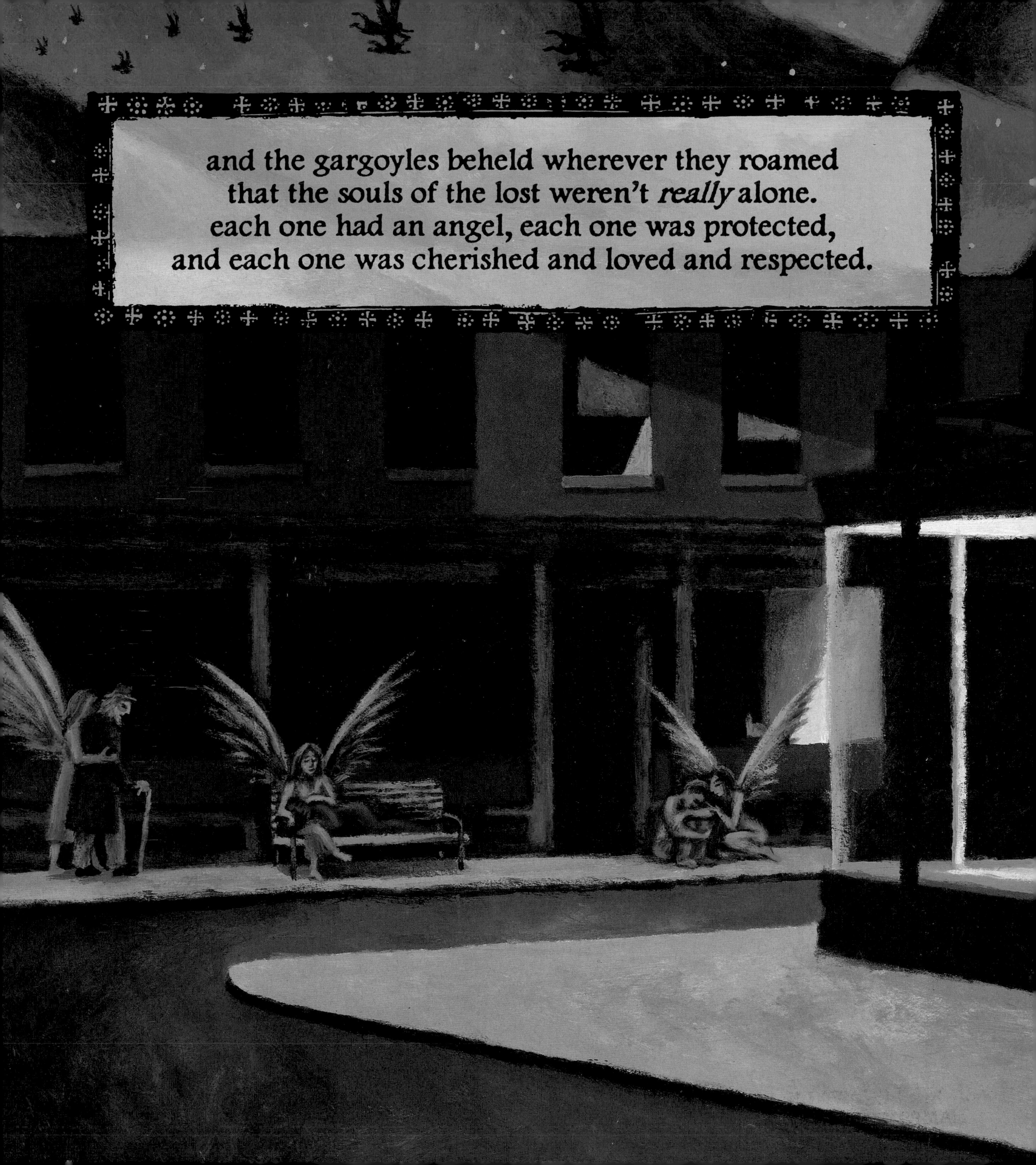
and the gargoyles beheld wherever they roamed
that the souls of the lost weren't *really* alone.
each one had an angel, each one was protected,
and each one was cherished and loved and respected.

PHILLIES

and so it is true with the gargoyles this day,
for all of the angels who love them have stayed.
and together they wait until days become nights,
to embark on their dark and most glorious flights.

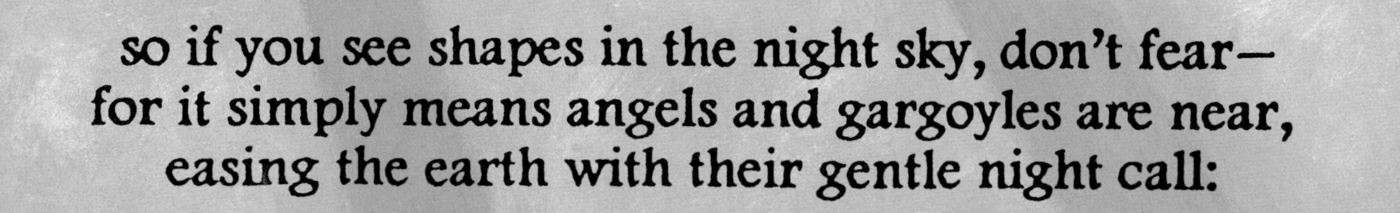
so if you see shapes in the night sky, don't fear—
for it simply means angels and gargoyles are near,
easing the earth with their gentle night call:

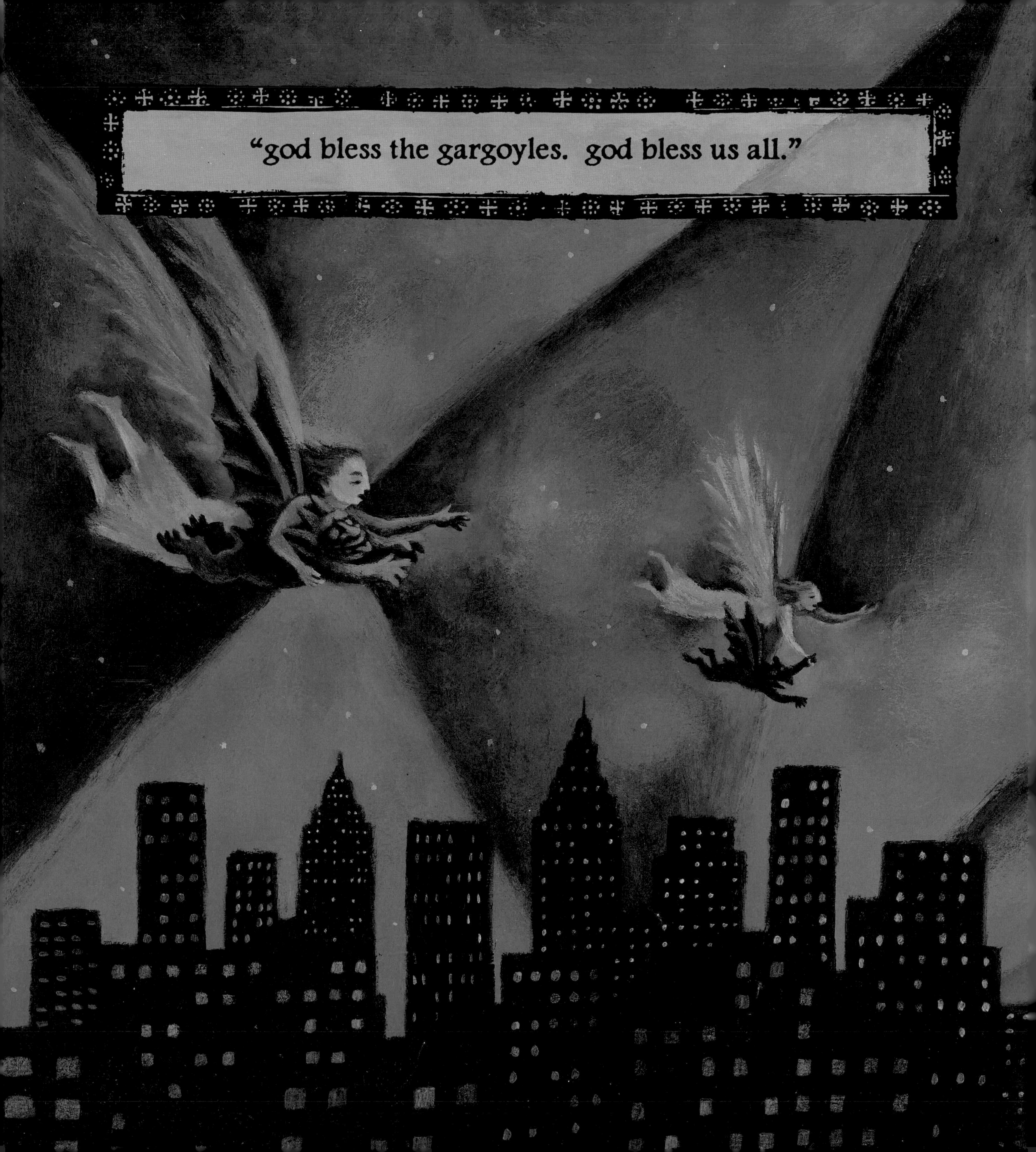
"god bless the gargoyles. god bless us all."